SILLY WILLY

Dedicated to my children and ever-growing number
of grandchildren. You are perfect just the way you are.

—S.M.

To my forever love and the one who
made me a mother. I love you.

—M.M.

ISBN 13: 978-1-4621-4247-7

Published by Sweetwater Books, an imprint of Cedar Fort, Inc.
2373 W. 700 S., Springville, UT 84663
Distributed by Cedar Fort, Inc., www.cedarfort.com

Library Of Congress Control Number: 2022933436

Cover design © 2022 Cedar Fort, Inc.

Printed in the United States of America

10 9 8 7 6 5 4 3 2 1

Printed on acid-free paper

SILLY WILLY

by Scott Mackintosh

illustrated by Mckenna Mackintosh

Sweetwater Books
An imprint of Cedar Fort, Inc.
Springville, Utah

This Book belongs to:

_____

A little frog named Willy
was acting very silly

as he thought about
the life of a frog.

His friends at school
had been real cruel

and told him it's
better being a dog.

"Mother," he pled, "change my name to Fred and throw me a toy or a bone.

"I'll run, and I'll fetch,

and the ball I will catch,
as quickly as it can be thrown."

His mom said to him with a
motherly grin,
"There's no joy in being a dog.

"Those fleas you would scratch and on your ears they would latch.

"No croaking from on top of a log.

"Sitting on a lily will
look pretty silly if
you insist on being a dog.

"You couldn't catch flies and
that's a big prize
in the wonderful life of a frog.

"You swim all the day and for you that is play

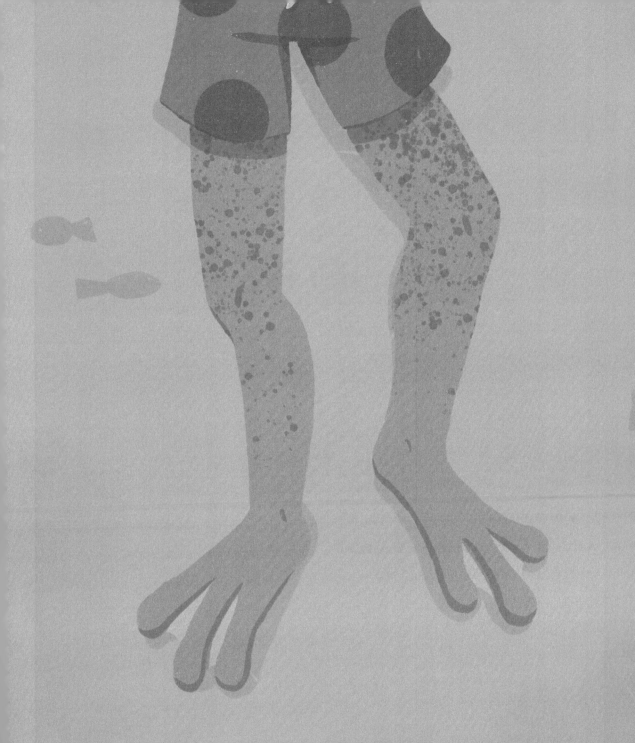

with your powerful legs
and webbed feet.

"You enjoy your nice pond
and I know you are fond

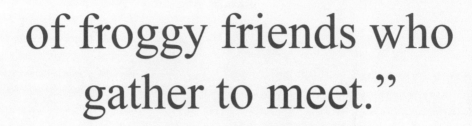

of froggy friends who
gather to meet."

That caused Willy to think as a
dog he would sink
if he tried sitting on top of a lily.

Life is good as a frog, so why be a dog? Looking back, it seemed awful silly.

"I was born what I am,
and I am a big fan.

"Most everyone would
have to agree.

I AM WILLY THE FROG!

"So, a frog I will stay, and
I won't go astray.

"For that's the BEST version of ME!"